The Last Smoker in America

Book and Lyrics by Bill Russell

Music by Peter Melnick

A SAMUEL FRENCH ACTING EDITION

SAMUEL FRENCH

FOUNDED 1830

SAMUELFRENCH.COM
SAMUELFRENCH-LONDON.CO.UK

FOR PRODUCTION ENQUIRIES

UNITED STATES AND CANADA
Info@SamuelFrench.com
1-866-598-8449

UNITED KINGDOM AND EUROPE
Plays@SamuelFrench-London.co.uk
020-7255-4302

Each title is subject to availability from Samuel French, depending upon country of performance. Please be aware that *THE LAST SMOKER IN AMERICA* may not be licensed by Samuel French in your territory. Professional and amateur producers should contact the nearest Samuel French office or licensing partner to verify availability.

MUSIC USE NOTE

Licensees are solely responsible for obtaining formal written permission from copyright owners to use copyrighted music in the performance of this play and are strongly cautioned to do so. If no such permission is obtained by the licensee, then the licensee must use only original music that the licensee owns and controls. Licensees are solely responsible and liable for all music clearances and shall indemnify the copyright owners of the play(s) and their licensing agent, Samuel French, against any costs, expenses, losses and liabilities arising from the use of music by licensees. Please contact the appropriate music licensing authority in your territory for the rights to any incidental music.

MUSIC MATERIALS

An orchestration will be loaned two months prior to the production ONLY on the receipt of the Licensing Fee quoted for all performances, the rental fee and a refundable deposit. Please contact Samuel French for perusal of the music materials as well as a performance license application.

The Original Cast Album for *THE LAST SMOKER IN AMERICA* is distributed by Yellow Sound Label and available on iTunes, Amazon, and elsewhere music is sold. For more information, visit Lastsmoker.com or YellowSoundLabel.com

IMPORTANT BILLING AND CREDIT REQUIREMENTS

If you have obtained performance rights to this title, please refer to your licensing agreement for important billing and credit requirements.

THE LAST SMOKER IN AMERICA received its world premiere at the Contemporary American Theatre Company in Columbus, Ohio (Steven Anderson, Artistic Director), opening on October 6, 2010. The production was directed by Andy Sandberg, with choreography by AC Ciulla, music supervision by Fred Lassen, sets by Charlie Corcoran, costumes by Michael McDonald, lighting by Jeff Croiter and Grant Yeager, and sound by Bart Fasbender. The cast was as follows:

PAM . . . . Katy Blake
PHYLLIS . . . . Natalie Venetia Belcon
ERNIE . . . . John Bolton
JIMMY . . . . Teddy Toye

THE LAST SMOKER IN AMERICA had its original Off Broadway production presented by Andy Sandberg, Whitney Hoagland Edwards, Michael Palitz, Stephanie Rosenberg, and Neal-rose Creations at the Westside Theatre (Roger Gindi, General Manager), opening on August 2, 2012, in New York. The production was directed by Andy Sandberg, with choreography by AC Ciulla, music supervision by Fred Lassen, lighting by Jeff Croiter and Grant Yeager, sets by Charlie Corcoran, costumes by Michael McDonald, and sound by Bart Fasbender. The cast was as follows:

PAM . . . . Farah Alvin
PHYLLIS . . . . Natalie Venetia Belcon
ERNIE . . . . John Bolton
JIMMY . . . . Jake Boyd

THE LAST SMOKER IN AMERICA was also presented in 2009 at the New York Musical Theatre Festival.

CHARACTERS

PAM – (30s to 50s)A disillusioned suburban mother and housewife, who teaches English Comp at a university. All she wants out of life is to have a cigarette in peace and quiet, but that grows increasingly impossible due to her family, which is anything but quiet or peaceful, and the increasingly draconian anti-smoking laws. Rebellious by nature, she refuses to take those laws lying down. She wants and strives to do the right thing, but after discovering her husband's infidelity and having an increasingly difficult time dealing with her hyperactive son, opts to smoke her last remaining cigarette. That choice means she will either go to prison or must go on the lam. Rock Voice.

ERNIE – (30s to 50s) A suburban father, recently let go from his job as an elementary school music teacher. Though he has quit smoking and tries to play by the rules, his dream is to be a rock star and he is constantly striving to write hit songs. His difficult teenage son is a constant source of irritation and the realities of marriage and adulthood have caused a mid-life crisis and anger management issues. He is growing increasingly distant from his wife. When she discovers he's been cheating on her and leaves, he becomes an anti-smoking zealot, losing all traces of the "rocker who knew how to party" he used to be. Rock Voice.

JIMMY – (teenager) A bright but difficult teenager without many friends, he loves his video games more than anything in the world, except rap music. He listens to so much of the latter he's convinced he's black. A prime example of someone with Attention Deficit Hyperactivity Disorder, he often forgets or refuses to take his medication. Though he and his father are constantly at loggerheads, he craves his dad's attention and approval. Not finding it, he often turns to his mother, but ultimately is left to make the 'grown up' decisions on his own. Pop/Rock Voice.

PHYLLIS – (30s to 50s) The eternally cheerful, Jesus-addicted, anti-smoking zealot who lives next door. Having given up smoking and affairs with married men, she is overbearing and vindictive. But she couches those tendencies in professions of universal love and charitable acts toward the sinners who still smoke. An African-American who secretly longs to be white, she is dismayed by Jimmy's wanting to be black. Gospel/Pop Voice.

SETTING

A suburban kitchen somewhere in America.

TIME

Tomorrow.

PROLOGUE

(ERNIE, a middle-aged wannabe rocker, enters and crosses to a microphone in front of the curtain.)

ERNIE. Hi, everyone. My name is Ernie. And I am powerless over nicotine.

VOICES. *(offstage)* Hi, Ernie.

ERNIE. This is my first Nic-A meeting. Like many of you, I recently quit smoking. It hasn't been easy, but with all the new laws I felt I had to. Truthfully, I'd probably sell my children for a couple puffs. Just kidding. I only have one child. A son. And I couldn't sell him. You can just have him. He's quite a handful – one of the reasons my wife, Pam, is having such a hard time.

WE ALL KNOW THE EVILS OF TOBACCO
I AM PROUD THAT I'M A MAN WHO QUIT
THOUGH MY WIFE KNOWS SMOKING IS A NO-NO
SHE TRIES TO STOP BUT SHE'S NOT GIVING UP THAT SHIT
SHE'S –

THE LAST SMOKER IN AMERICA
IF ONLY SHE COULD FIND ANOTHER HIGH
THE LAST SMOKER IN AMERICA
THERE ARE THOSE WHO SAY THAT SHE SHOULD FRY
YES SHE'S
THE LAST SMOKER IN AMERICA
I WISH THAT SHE WOULD KISS THOSE BUTTS GOODBYE

(ERNIE exits as curtain opens on –)

(Time: Tomorrow. Early morning.)

(Place: A suburban kitchen. Doors to the living room, basement and a broom closet. A dinette set to one side is balanced by an island counter on which sits a kitschy cookie jar.)

(PAM, a middle-aged housewife wearing a bathrobe, surreptitiously takes out a cigarette and smells it lovingly, looks around furtively, then takes out a lighter. Suddenly, a high-tech device on the wall crackles to life with beeps and buzzes, frightening **PAM** *and causing her to drop the cigarette.)*

PAM. AAHHH! What the hell?!

ASPHYXIA SYSTEM. *(offstage voice) (a chirpy female voice)* Thank you for purchasing your ASPHYXIA system.

PAM. ASPHYXIA?

ASPHYXIA SYSTEM. *(offstage voice)* My name is an acronym for Anti-Smoking Penalty Help You Xpect In America. The penalties for smoking remain unchanged: heavy fines and social ostracism. But new and stricter laws, including jail time, are expected any minute.

(singing a jaunty jingle)

HAVE A VERY NICE
TOBACCO-FREE DAY

PAM. Stricter laws? Jail time? How did this happen?!

(Music in, as **PAM** *puts the cigarette she's holding back into the pack. As she starts to sing she crosses to the cookie jar and buries the pack under some cookies.)*

[*"HOW CAN I QUIT NOW?"*]

I'M INTELLIGENT AND STABLE
I DON'T NEED TO SMOKE
I AM EMINENTLY ABLE
TO JOIN THE RIGHTEOUS FOLK
IF I CONTEMPLATE THIS TABLE
AND OTHER DINETTE SETS
MY MIND WILL NOT GO DRIFTING
TO WHERE I HID MY CIGARETTES

I'M CONTROLLING MY SICK URGES
ANY WAY I CAN
DETERMINATION PURGES
MUCH BETTER THAN A BAN
I WILL NOT FEED THIS COMPULSION

I WILL SIMPLY COOL MY JETS
NO WAY WILL I BE FLYING
TO WHERE I HID MY CIGARETTES

WHO AM I KIDDING?
CIGARETTES FILL A VOID
SO WHO AM I KIDDING?
MY LIFE'S A HEMORRHOID
I HAVE GOT TO KICK THIS HABIT
I HAVE MADE A SOLEMN VOW
BUT HOW CAN I QUIT NOW?

(**ERNIE** *enters, a middle-aged hippie/slacker – unkempt hair, well-worn jeans, distressed rocker t-shirt, maybe his electric guitar hanging from a strap around his neck. He is on edge.*)

ERNIE. Are we out of nicotine gum?

PAM. Sorry, honey. I ate the last carton when I got up this morning.

ERNIE. *(taking an energy drink from fridge)* Damn it, Sweetie, how the hell do you expect me to look for a job without gum?

(goes to punch the wall)

PAM. Anger management, Ernie. Not the wall. The clown! The clown!

(**PAM** *rushes to get a big inflatable clown and sets it in front of* **ERNIE**, *who punches it like a mad man.*)

Feel better?

ERNIE. I hate that fuckin' clown.

PAM. Where the hell did that talking and singing contraption come from?

ERNIE. The ASPHYXIA? I installed it last night.

PAM. It scared the hell out of me.

ERNIE. It's meant to. I'll employ any tool I can to help us lick this – including fear.

PAM. Fear makes me want to smoke.

ERNIE.

    PAM! PAM! PAM!
    I WONDER IF YOU GIVE A DAMN
    ABOUT THE HEALTH
    OF YOUR HUSBAND AND YOUR SON
    OR THE DAMAGE THAT IS DONE
    WHEN YOU POLLUTE OUR AIR
    I SURE HOPE YOU'RE HAVING FUN
    YOU ARE PLAYING WITH OUR FATE
    WE MIGHT HAVE TO RELOCATE
    ON THE RUN FROM UNCLE SAM
    WHILE THE ZEALOTS AIM THEIR HATE
    AT THE SMOKER KNOWN AS PAM!
    Good-bye.

PAM. Good-bye?

ERNIE. I'm going to get some gum.

PAM. Whew. I thought you were leaving me.

ERNIE. Would that scare you into quitting? I'll leave and you can have Jimmy?

PAM. NO!

    (**ERNIE** *exits as* **JIMMY**, **PAM** *and* **ERNIE**'*s teenage son, enters rapidly, playing a game on his cell phone during the following.*)

JIMMY. MAAAAA!!! Can I have a cookie?

PAM. Jimmy, you'll be late for school.

JIMMY. Not going. School's boring.

PAM. Honey, I don't have time for this argument today. I have to fight my cravings.

JIMMY. I can help. I'm the best fighter in the Universe – the Master Thug of Gongazeth!

PAM. Life is not a video game. You can help by going to school.

JIMMY. *(erupting)* I'M NOT FRIGGIN' GOING TO FRIGGIN' SCHOOL! *(instantly super sweet)* Can I have a cookie?

PAM. No! Sugar makes you hyper.

JIMMY.

    MA
    COME ON
    I REALLY WANT A COOKIE

                    PAM. No.

    I'VE BEEN PRETTY GOOD
    AND I DESERVE A TREAT

                  No, Jimmy.

    I HAVE A MONSTER
       CRAVING
    TO EAT SOMETHING
       THAT'S SWEET

                  Not now!

    I THINK I NEED A COOKIE
    'CAUSE I'M FEELING KINDA
       BLAH
    SO COME ON
    JUST ONE FRIGGIN' COOKIE
    MA

PAM. Well, I guess one cookie couldn't hurt. But don't tell your father I gave it to you.

JIMMY. *(manically jumping around)* I gotta cookie! I gotta cookie!

PAM. Did you take your medication?

JIMMY. Yes.

PAM. When?

JIMMY. Like I'm supposed to remember?

PAM. When you got up? With your breakfast?

JIMMY. HOW THE HELL SHOULD I KNOW WHEN I TOOK MY STUPID PILLS??!!

PAM. You seem a little jumpy.

JIMMY. HORMONES!!!

(He slams out of the kitchen as **PHYLLIS**, *a super upbeat neighbor who is African-American, enters.)*

PHYLLIS. Morning, neighbor. What a blessedly beautiful day!

PAM. Phyllis? You're up early.

PHYLLIS. So much going on – the big event tonight and new anti-smoking laws expected any minute!

PAM. Sorry. No time to talk. I'm late for a student conference.

PHYLLIS.

> PAMMIE SWEETIE
> I NEED A HAND
> YOU CAN'T TELL ME YOU'RE TOO BUSY
> MAN THE TRENCHES
> THIS IS WARTIME!
>
> PAMMIE HONEY
> YOU UNDERSTAND
> WE HAVE GOT TO BAND TOGETHER
> AND THEN FIGHT LIKE KNIGHTS OF YORE
> NICOTINE IS KNOCKING AT THE DOOR
> CARCINOGINS ARE SEEPING
> INTO EACH AND EV'RY PORE!

PAM. Phyllis, I'm well aware of the evils of tobacco. I just don't have time right now to…

PHYLLIS.

> OH AND PAMMIE!
> I'VE GOT BIG NEWS
> I'M ABOUT TO BE APPOINTED
> AS OUR DISTRICT'S NO-SMOKE CAPTAIN
> SUCH AN HONOR
> I'VE PAID MY DUES
> BUT THE TITLE COMES WITH DUTIES
> AND MEANS EVEN MORE TO DO
> THERE'S A HOLY MISSION TO PURSUE
> PAM! TO FIGHT THE EVILS OF TOBACCO
> I NEED YOU
> WILL YOU HELP ME?

> (**ERNIE** and **JIMMY** emerge from the cabinets and refrigerator and join **PHYLLIS** – the needy voices in **PAM**'s head.)

ERNIE.	JIMMY.	PHYLLIS.
PAM		
	MA	
		PAMELA
GUM		
	COOKIE	
		HELP
DO NOT PUT US IN A FIX	I'M FEELING KINDA BLAH	
FOR YOUR CHEAP KICKS		
		I COULD REALLY USE YOUR HELP
PAM		
	MA	
		PAMELA
GUM		
	COOKIE	
		HELP
DO NOT PUT US IN A FIX	I'M FEELING FAINT AND KINDA BLAH	
IT'S TIME TO NIX		I COULD
THOSE CHEAP KICKS	SWEETS WOULD HELP	USE YOUR HELP
PAM	MA	PAMELA

PAM. *(covering her ears, trying to block out their voices)*
I JUST WANT TO SMOKE
IN PEACE AND QUIET
NO INTERRUPTIONS OR REQUESTS
MY HARD-EARNED RELIEF
FROM LIFE'S DAILY RIOT
MAKES ME A PARIAH

EVERYONE DETESTS
SO SMOKING LEADS
TO HEART-ACHE AND CRAPPINESS
AND TO PRECIPITOUS DECLINE
HOW I PURSUE
MY OWN HAPPINESS
IS NOBODY'S BUSINESS BUT MINE

(**ERNIE, JIMMY** and **PHYLLIS** create a cacophony of pleas.)

	JIMMY.	
	MA!	**PHYLLIS.**
ERNIE.		PAMELA!
HONEY, HONEY		
		PAMELA!
	MA!	
HOW COULD YOU EAT THE GUM?		
	CAN I PLEASE HAVE A COOKIE?	
		I REALLY NEED YOUR HELP!
HOW COULD YOU EAT THE GUM,	CAN I HAVE A COOKIE	I NEED HELP
PAM?	MA?	PAMELA!

PAM.	**ERNIE, JIMMY, PHYLLIS.**
MY HUSBAND, SON AND NEIGHBOR	HELP ME
CAN EASILY PROVOKE	ME ME ME
MY MARRIAGE, HOME AND LABOR	NEED HELP
ALL MAKE ME WANT TO SMOKE	LOOK SEE?
I WILL NOT FEED THIS COMPULSION	I'M NEEDY

I WILL SIMPLY COOL MY
    JETS

AS CAN BE

PAM.
NO WAY
    WILL
I BE FLYING
TO HIDDEN
CIGARETTES,
    NO

PHYLLIS.
IT'S TIME
    TO QUIT
YOU GOTTA
    QUIT

ERNIE.

HAVE TO
    QUIT
I'M OVER IT,
    PAM

GONNA DO
    IT
GONNA
    QUIT
    NOW

JIMMY.

CAN'T YOU
    SEE
    THAT
I NEED   I NEED
    HELP   HELP
         HERE
HERE
GIMME,   GIMME,   GIMME,
    GIMME   GIMME   GIMME

I CAN DO
    IT!

ERNIE, JIMMY, PHYLLIS.
WHO ARE YOU KIDDING?

PAM.
JUNKIES CAN'T INSTRUCT

WHO ARE YOU KIDDING?

I'M COMPLETELY FUCKED!
I HAVE GOT TO KICK THIS
    HABIT
I HAVE MADE A SOLEMN
    VOW

OOH, LA, LA

OOH, LA, LA, LA, QUIT

BUT HOW CAN I QUIT NOW?	SO QUIT, YOU MUST, YOU'D BETTER QUIT NOW
HOW, HOW, HOW? HOW CAN I QUIT NOW?	HOW, HOW, HOW? NOW!

*(**ERNIE**, **JIMMY** and **PHYLLIS** exit back into the cabinets and refrigerator as **PAM** crosses to the cookie jar. She digs furiously in it, throwing out handfuls of cookies. Then she pulls out the mangled cigarette pack. It holds the ultimate prize – one that hasn't been touched.)*

PAM. Noooooooo! *(Puts the cigarette pack back in the cookie jar. Tries to talk herself out of her need.)* I will not smoke. I will not smoke. I...WILL...NOT...SMOKE!

ASPHYXIA SYSTEM. *(offstage voice)* Attention! Anti-smoking law update. Possession of even a single cigarette can now be punished by up to a year in jail.

PAM. A single cigarette?

(She retrieves the cigarette pack and puts it in her bathrobe pocket.)

ASPHYXIA SYSTEM. *(offstage voice)*
HAVE A VERY NICE
TOBACCO-FREE DAY

JIMMY. *(entering)* Can I have another cookie?

PAM. *(yelling at him)* NOOOO!!

JIMMY. Whoa, Ma, are you sure you want to give up smoking? It evens you out.

PAM. Jimmy, if I don't kick the habit, I could go to jail.

JIMMY. Can I go too? All my favorite rappers have been there.

PAM. It's jail, Jimmy. Not music camp.

JIMMY. YOU NEVER LET ME HAVE ANY FUN!

PHYLLIS. *(entering)* Jimmy? Shouldn't you be in school?

JIMMY. Mind your own friggin' business, lady!

PAM. Don't say "friggin'", Jimmy.

JIMMY. Why the fuck not? Gotta go – the Avatar of Megalon must be stopped.

PHYLLIS. I'll pray for you, Jimmy.

JIMMY. Yeah. Whatever.

(exits)

PHYLLIS. Pam, I really need you. I've barely assumed the title of our district's No-Smoke Captain and I'm positively overwhelmed with all the responsibility. Can you help me tonight?

PAM. Tonight? What's tonight?

PHYLLIS. Are you okay? The Annual Tobacco Burn?! With the new laws we're expecting a record turn-out. You will be there?

PAM. I don't know, Phyllis. I've been so busy at school. I can't seem to get motivated. About anything. And just the thought of smelling all that smoke…

PHYLLIS. I understand. When I first quit I couldn't go to the Burn either. But I promise you – some day you'll be dancing around that bonfire.

PAM. I can't wait for that day.

PHYLLIS. How's that going?

PAM. Smoking?

PHYLLIS. Quitting.

PAM. Of course! Well…very well! I won't pretend it's not hard.

PHYLLIS. I know. But you can lick it. Look how well Ernie's doing.

PAM. Is he?

PHYLLIS. Oh yes! As his sponsor I can attest he's a new man since he quit smoking.

PAM. I haven't noticed. The slightest little thing sets him off. Just this morning he nearly punched a hole in the wall because I ate all the nicotine gum. And quitting hasn't helped him find a job.

PHYLLIS. I have complete confidence in him. If you want to join the reformed you should use my method.

PAM. What method?

PHYLLIS. Jesus.

PAM. Of course.

PHYLLIS. Put your faith in Him and you'll never want another cigarette. They're Satan's playthings, you know?

PAM. I didn't.

PHYLLIS. Well, just look at who uses them – terrorists, pornographers, the French! And why do you think hell is portrayed as a place of fire?

PAM. You can always get a light?

PHYLLIS. Hell is portrayed as a place of fire and brimstone because even in Jesus's time that's where all the smokers were sent.

PAM. Really? I didn't know they smoked back then.

PHYLLIS. Oh yes – it's in Scripture. *(about to quote chapter and verse, then covering)* Somewhere.

["LET THE LORD BE YOUR ADDICTION"]

I HAD A BAD TOBACCO HABIT
FOUR PACKS A DAY OR MORE
I WAS FRIGHTENED AS A RABBIT
BY A LOUD KNOCK AT MY DOOR
BUT I OPENED IT TO JESUS
WHO GLOWED WITH INNER LIGHT
HE CHANGED MY CIGGIES INTO SNACKS
AND RESTORED MY APPETITE

LET THE LORD BE YOUR ADDICTION
LET HIM FILL YOUR LUNGS WITH HOPE
TELL THE DEVIL, "GET BEHIND ME
I'VE GOT JESUS AS MY DOPE"
WHEN I SMOKED THE ANGELS SCREAMED
"YOU SLUTTY CONCUBINE"
LET THE LORD BE YOUR ADDICTION
AS I HAVE MADE HIM MINE

WHILE WE ALL HAVE OUR OWN ADDICTIONS
MOST OF WHICH ARE WICKED BAD

YOU CAN NEVER GET TOO MUCH OF
THE BALM IN GILEAD
YOU COULD NEVER OVERDOSE ON EXTRA PIETY
IF JESUS WAS MADE INTO PILLS
HE'D BE TRIPLE ECSTACY!

I know you hear what I'm saying, Pamela. I've always felt such support from you and your family for my mission.

PAM. You have?

PHYLLIS. Oh, yes. In my mind we're all one big happy clan – like the Osmond Family!

(**ERNIE** and **JIMMY** *enter through the cabinets wearing sequined jumpsuits. They join* **PAM** *to become the Osmond Family back-up singers* **PHYLLIS** *thinks of them as.*)

PHYLLIS.	**ERNIE, JIMMY.**
	WHEEE-OO! YEAH-AH!
LET THE LORD BE YOUR ADDICTION	GO, GOD, GO
LET JESUS BE YOUR FIX	GO WITH GOD
LET THE HOLY SPIRIT SHOW YOU	GO, GOD, GO
BETTER WAYS TO GET YOUR KICKS	YAY, GOD!
IF YOU'RE GONNA BE A JUNKIE	OOOOOO
WHY CHOOSE SMOKE OR CRACK OR WINE	WHY
LET THE LORD BE YOUR ADDICTION	LET THE LORD BE YOUR ADDICTION
AS I HAVE MADE HIM MINE!	

Osmond Brothers and Sister, I am here to testify!

ERNIE, JIMMY. Testify!

PHYLLIS. I was a sinful smoker!

But then I replaced my tobacco jones
with my love for the bones of Jeeesus!

ERNIE, PAM, JIMMY. Amen!

PHYLLIS. So if you need a smoke? *(cuing her backup)*

PHYLLIS, ERNIE, PAM, JIMMY. Smoke Jesus!

PHYLLIS. If you crave a toke?

PHYLLIS, ERNIE, PAM, JIMMY. Toke Jesus!

PHYLLIS. If you're into coke?

PHYLLIS, ERNIE, PAM, JIMMY. Snort Jesus!

PHYLLIS.

YES THE LORD WILL BE YOUR FIX!

PHYLLIS.	**ERNIE, JIMMY, PAM**.
LET THE LORD BE YOUR ADDICTION	GO, GOD, GO
LET JESUS LIFT YOUR CURSE	GO WITH GOD
BEING DRIVEN TO TOBACCO	GO, GOD, GO
IS LIKE DRIVING YOUR OWN HEARSE	YAY, GOD!
IF YOU'RE GONNA BE A JUNKIE	
WHY CHOOSE SMOKE OR CRACK OR WINE	CRACK OR WINE
LET THE LORD BE YOUR ADDICTION	
AS I HAVE MADE HIM MINE!	
LET THE LORD BE YOUR ADDICTION	LET THE LORD BE YOUR ADDICTION
AS I HAVE MADE HIM MINE!	AS I HAVE MADE HIM MINE!

*(At end of song, **PHYLLIS** leaves as **ERNIE** and **JIMMY** exit through the cabinets. **PAM** crosses to the cookie jar and takes out the cigarette pack. Inside is an un-touched cigarette. Digging deeper, she finds a stub. **PAM** talks to these prized possessions like a little girl playing with dolls.)*

PAM. This little ciggie is my baby. And this big ciggie is my hero, because you'll be there for me when I need you most. I wouldn't even think of smoking you now. You're one of the last of your species in this country and I will protect you to the end. *(to stub)* But you, my precious ciggie stub, are Mommy's little helper and I can hear you saying, "I taste so good."

(Happily, she lights the stub. Then, hearing ERNIE offstage, jumps into the broom closet.)

ERNIE. *(offstage)* Honey? I'm back.

(ERNIE enters the kitchen, carrying a shopping bag and a long package.)

Honey? I'm back. I got the gum. They were out of Spearmint so I thought we'd try the Nacho Cheese. *(Sniffing the air, putting the packages on the table)* Honey?

(Continues sniffing. The scent leads him to the broom closet. He pauses, then yanks open the door. Smoke pours out.)

Aha! I knew it! You haven't quit, have you? Where are they?

PAM. I have quit, Ernie! I just…get so anxious and down in the dumps. I think it's those pills we've been taking to quit.

ERNIE. They worked for me.

PAM. I've read they can lead to depression – even suicide. And you have seemed depressed for the last…ten years or so.

ERNIE. *(taking an energy drink from the fridge)* I'm not depressed. Just frustrated that my wife loves tobacco more than me.

PAM. Anger management!

(ERNIE pulls the clown from pantry, punches it, and kicks it back in.)

I do not love tobacco more than I love you. No more than you love those energy drinks. You know, the law banning the jumbo versions of those was not meant to encourage you to down four or five smaller ones every hour!

ERNIE. Don't change the subject! If you really cared about your family you wouldn't expose us to second-hand cancer. Face it, Pam, you're an add –

PAM. Do not use the A word with me! Ever!

ERNIE. Acknowledging your problem – is the first step.

PAM. I don't have a problem. I could quit. I'm just under a lot of stress. My English Comp students can't focus on any piece of writing longer than a tweet.

ERNIE. I have my own issues. I really need to write a hit song for my garage band.

PAM. We don't have a garage. You *really* need to get a job.

ERNIE. I have a job – I'm a rocker.

PAM. I meant a job that pays. How long am I gonna be the sole support of our family?

(**ERNIE**'s *face crumbles.*)

I'm sorry, honey. I didn't mean –

ERNIE. Those little bastards just didn't appreciate my genius.

PAM. Your third graders loved you! Their parents objected to you teaching them to sing "The Bitch is Back".

ERNIE. That was just an excuse. They really fired me because they smelled your smoke on my clothes!

(**PHYLLIS** *enters.*)

PHYLLIS. Oh, Ernie, so glad you're here. When I was talking to Pam, I forgot to ask…Wait. Do I smell…smoke?

PAM. Smoke? No! Oh – that's probably the barbecue – Ernie was grilling.

PHYLLIS. Grilling? Breakfast?

ERNIE. I just love…barbecued eggs.

PAM. What do you need, Phyllis?

PHYLLIS. I was so focused on getting you to the Burn that I forgot to ask if Ernie will be there. And if he would play some of his songs?

ERNIE. Wouldn't miss it, Phyllis – one of my favorite gigs.

PHYLLIS. Wonderful! Music has such a calming effect on all those edgy junkies. Gotta run!

(exits)

ERNIE. Where are they? The cigarettes. Where did you hide them?

PAM. That was the end. I kept a stub. Not even half a stub.

ERNIE. Hand it over, Pam!

*(**ERNIE** holds out his hand. Reluctantly, **PAM** gives him the stub. He rips it to pieces.)*

I thought when your smoking caused us to lose our health insurance it would make an impression. Our entire life's savings have gone to anti-smoking fines! *(He surreptitiously smells the tobacco on his fingers.)* Honey, I know you're having a very hard time so – I got a little present for my sweetie. Look!

(unwraps the long package with a flourish, revealing a shotgun)

PAM. A rifle?!

ERNIE. No. A shotgun!

PAM. I guess blowing my brains out is one way to quit.

ERNIE. You don't appreciate the intensity of hatred out there for people like you. When you lapse again – IF you lapse again – I'll employ this rifle to defend you to the end!

PAM. Oh, what have we come to!? How did this happen?! Guns?! Jail time?!

ERNIE. *(breaking down)* Oh god! That smoke smelled so fuckin' good. Why do you have to bring temptation into the house?

PAM. I'm sorry. So, so sorry.

ERNIE. Why did it all go bad?

PAM. I went bad.

ERNIE. When I think of everything we used to experiment with – weed…

(During the following list, **PAM** *reacts vocally to each item* **ERNIE** *mentions.)*

Mushrooms. Acid. Cocaine. Quaaludes. Opium…

PAM. I never did opium. You tried it without me?!

ERNIE. Well – cigarettes seemed relatively harmless. Why can't it be like when we met? I saw you across that smoky bar and I knew.

PAM. What did you know, honey?

ERNIE. That I wanted…wanted to light your cigarette.

["HANGIN' OUT IN A SMOKY BAR"]

ERNIE.
WAS THAT THE BEST PART
   OF OUR YOUTH?

> **PAM.** Everyone lit up back then.

I CAN'T RECALL FEELING
   MORE ALIVE

> So what if it was killing us?

THE ATMOSPHERE ROWDY
   AND UNCOUTH

> The glowing tips of all those cigarettes looked like little fire-flies.

BUT NOTHING COULD
   BEAT THAT LOCAL DIVE

(The cabinets open and a cigarette machine slides on. There is a neon sign above it and a lot of smoke. The island swivels around to reveal a restaurant booth. **PAM** *and* **ERNIE** *sit across from each other.)*

ERNIE & PAM.
HANGIN' OUT IN A SMOKY BAR
TALKIN' LATE INTO THE NIGHT
SALTED PEANUTS WERE CAVIAR
AS WE BASKED IN THE GLOW OF RED NEON LIGHT

PAM.
    SERVICE WAS SLOW AND NOT TOO POLITE

ERNIE.
    THE MUSIC WAS HOT AND
        WE WERE COOL

                    PAM. Rock stars would smoke while performing a song.

    NOBODY THOUGHT ABOUT
        BLACK LUNG

                    Doctors would smoke while performing surgery.

    WE LOVED TO CHALLENGE
        EV'RY RULE

                    I would even smoke while performing fellatio.

ERNIE & PAM.
    LIFE WAS SO GREAT WHEN WE WERE YOUNG!

    HANGIN' OUT IN A SMOKY BAR
    DIDN'T HAVE MUCH SENSE OR BREAD

PAM.
    YOU WOULD STRUM ON YOUR OLD GUITAR
    AND YOUR FINGERS WOULD PLAY WHAT HAD GONE UNSAID

ERNIE.
    I WAS TRYING TO SAY "CAN WE GO TO BED?"

ERNIE & PAM.
    AND THAT LED TO THE DAY WE WED

    WE WOULD IMBIBE 'TIL OUR EYES WOULD GLAZE
    AND PLAN HOW WE'D SET THE WORLD ABLAZE
    OH TO GO BACK TO THOSE CAREFREE DAYS
    WE LOOKED MUCH BETTER THROUGH A HAZE

    (They kiss as booth, neon sign and smoke disappear.)

ERNIE.
    THAT FUNKY HANG-OUT IS
        LONG GONE

                PAM.
                    LIKE SO MUCH WE LOVED

ERNIE. NOW THERE'S A SPA
WITH HEALTHY GRUB

> **PAM.**
>
> I HATE HEALTHY GRUB

THOUGH WE'VE GROWN UP
AND WE'VE MOVED ON

PAM.

DO YOU THINK WE'VE GROWN?
I WISH WE WERE BACK IN THAT OLD PUB

ERNIE. Me too, babe.

ERNIE & PAM.

HANGIN' OUT IN A SMOKY BAR
NOW IT SEEMS SO LONG AGO
THOUGH WE HAVEN'T GONE VERY FAR
WE NO LONGER RECALL WHAT WE USED TO KNOW
WHEN THE TEMPO OF LIFE WAS ADAGIO

PAM.

WHEN WE HAD TIME TO SPARE AND WE TOOK IT SLOW

PAM & ERNIE.

HANGIN' OUT IN A SMOKY BAR
HANGIN' OUT IN A SMOKY BAR

*(**ERNIE** exits to basement as **JIMMY** enters in full rapper gear.)*

JIMMY. S'up?

PAM. Sup? You want supper? It's not even lunchtime.

JIMMY. Where Dad at? Gimme the 411.

PAM. You want to make a call, use your own phone.

JIMMY. The 411? The info? On Dad? He my Nigga.

PAM. Jimmy! Don't say that!

JIMMY. Say what?

PAM. The N word.

JIMMY. Why not?

PAM. It's terrible. It's discriminatory. I know those rappers you listen to use it, but they're black.

JIMMY. Yo, mamma. I be the blackest Nigga on the block.

PAM. Except for Phyllis this is an all-white neighborhood. Which is not why we chose it!

(ERNIE enters from basement.)

ERNIE. Honey, I think it's better if I keep the…you-know-what in the basement.

JIMMY. What? I don't know what.

ERNIE. This doesn't concern you, son.

JIMMY. Sho nuf does. We be family.

PAM. He right – we be…we are family. We need to include him more. Jimmy, your father has deemed it necessary to turn our home into an arsenal.

(showing him the shotgun)

JIMMY. *(grabbing it from her)* Aaawwww, sheee-it. Kewl. Hey, dad? Can I shoot this?

ERNIE. No, Jimmy. This is not a toy. This is dangerous.

JIMMY. *(whining)* But, Dad! *(now in a "street" style voice)* You my…

(catching a fierce look from PAM)

Negro.

(music in)

ERNIE. What the hell?

[*"GANGSTA"*]

JIMMY. I had a dream that I be black. Blackety black black black black. Uh. Uh huh. Check it out. Straight out of Compton, y'all. Here we go.
FUCK THE WORLD OF WHITEY
THAT SHIT AIN'T FOR ME
MY HOME IN THE GHETTO
WHERE THE BROTHERS BE

I TAKE MY REMY NECTAR
WITH A NYMPHOMANIAC
I GOT A BULL SHIT DETECTOR
'CAUSE I BE BLACK

PAM. Jimmy, please stop saying you're black. Phyllis could pop in at any minute.

JIMMY. In my dream Phyllis be my scratcher.

(**PHYLLIS** *appears as a thugged-out D.J. covered in bling. She works turntables to accompany* **JIMMY***'s fantasy.*)

FIRST THING IN THE MORNIN'
IN MY LOOKIN' GLASS
I REALIZE HOW MUCH
I'M LOVIN' MY BLACK ASS
MY BODY IS A TOTAL AFRO-DISIAK
AND ALL MY HOMIES LOVE ME
'CAUSE I BE BLACK
I BE BLACK

(*At first* **ERNIE** *and* **PAM***'s responses are out of the rhythm* **JIMMY** *has established.*)

PAM. No.

ERNIE. You are not.

JIMMY.

YEAH I BE BLACK!

PAM. You are not.

ERNIE. Listen to your mother.

JIMMY.

YO, YO
I A GANGSTA

ERNIE. Oh no!

PAM. You're in high school.

JIMMY.

YEAH, HO
I THE ILLEST!

PAM. Oh, honey, you're not feeling well?

ERNIE. I'm not feeling well!

JIMMY.

I SAY I A GANGSTA
WITH MY AK-47
I A LETHAL WARLORD
GONNA SHOOT MY WAY TO HEAVEN

    I GOT SOME STICKY DIGITS
    GONNA GRAB A BUNCH O' RICHES
    I A GANGSTA
    I BE CATNIP TO THE BITCHES!

    ROLLIN' DOWN THE STREET
    YOU DON'T KNOW WHAT I PACKIN'
    GOT THE DOPEST BEAT
    AIN'T NOTHIN' I LACKIN'   **PHYLLIS.**

                  NOTHIN' HE LACKIN'

PAM. Nothing you're lacking? How about good grammar?

    (**PAM** *and* **ERNIE** *start falling into* **JIMMY***'s rhythm.*)

    YOU'RE A WHITE BOY FROM SUBURBIA

ERNIE.

    ABOUT AS BLACK AS IRAQ OR SERBIA

PAM.

    FULL OF PETULANCE AND PERTURBIA

ERNIE & PAM.

    JUST A WHITE BOY FROM SUBURBIA!

JIMMY.

    YOU A CRACKER!
    YOU BOF CRACKERS!!!
    I A GANGSTA!
    Just ask my homies!

    (*to audience*)

    IF YOU RECKANIZE SAY "HEY"

PHYLLIS. (*cuing the audience to respond*) "HEY"

JIMMY.

    IF YOU THINK I'M CHILL SAY "HO"

PHYLLIS. (*cueing audience*) "HO"

JIMMY.

    IF YOU DIGGIN' MY SWAG SAY "YO"

PHYLLIS. (*leading audience*) "YO"

JIMMY.

    IF WHAT I'M SPITTIN' BE ILL SAY "GO"

PHYLLIS. *(with audience)* "GO"

JIMMY.

> HEY

PHYLLIS. *(leading the audience on each response)*

> HEY

JIMMY.

> HO

PHYLLIS. *(with audience)*

> HO

JIMMY.

> YO

PHYLLIS. *(leading audience)*

> YO

JIMMY.

> GO

PHYLLIS. *(with audience)*

> GO!

JIMMY.

> SUPERMAN THAT HO!

> (**JIMMY** *goes wild in a dance break. Then he goes for the shotgun.*)

ERNIE. *(taking rifle from him)* Touch that gun again and it's the end of your allowance.

JIMMY.

I CAN HANDLE YO PIECE	**ERNIE.**
	YOUR ALLOWANCE
	DECREASES
I CAN HANDLE YO NIECE	**PAM.**
	WE DON'T HAVE ANY
	NIECES
I GOTTA SLAMMIN' RIDE	
	YOU CAN'T DRIVE
MY BLING IS B-B-B-B-	
BONAFIDE	**ERNIE.**
	JIVE!
FUCK NO!	

YO, YO, WATCH ME SLIDE

PAM.
SLIDE TO SCHOOL!

I A THUG!

ERNIE.
YOU'RE A FOOL!

BETTER CHECK THE DATE

PHYLLIS.

BETTER CHECK THE CLOCK CLOCK

'CAUSE I THE BIGGEST

   MOTHER… BEEP!

ON THE BLOCK

PAM.

OH NO!

JIMMY.

OH YEAH! OH YEAH!

PAM.

OH NO!

THAT'S NOT A PLACE YOU WANNA GO

TAKE YOUR BEAT DOWN THAT STREET

YOU'RE BOUND TO TAKE A FALL

'CAUSE YOU'RE LOOKIN'

PAM.

AT YOUR

   MOTHER

         ERNIE.   **JIMMY.**

           WHAT?   WHA?

I'M THE ONLY

   MOTHER

           WHAT?   WHA?

I'M THE BIGGEST

   MOTHER OF

   THEM ALL

JIMMY.

GO, MOTHER, GO!

              ERNIE.

              STOP

JIMMY.

GO

　　　　　　　　STOP

GO

　　　　　　　　STOP

GO

　　　　　　　　STOP

GO

　　　　　　　　STOP
　　　　　　　　SHE'S YOUR MOTHER
　　　　　　　　I'M YOUR POP

YOU A HONKEY

PHYLLIS.

SNAP!

JIMMY.	**PAM..**	**ERNIE.**
OHHHHHHHH		OHHHHHHHHH
	LOOKIN'	
	AT YOUR	
	MOTHER	
GO		
	YEAH I'M	
	THE ONLY	
	MOTHER	
		STOP
	I'M THE BIGGEST	
	MOTHER ON	
	THE BLOCK	
GO		
		STOP
	YOU'RE LOOKIN'	
	AT	
GO	YOUR MOTHER	STOP
GO	I IS NOT YOUR	STOP
	BROTHER	
	I'M THE BIGGEST	
	MOTHER ON	
	THE BLOCK	
GO		
		STOP

JIMMY.
> YOU BOF CRACKERS!
> BIG OLE SALTINES!!!
> I SAY I A GANGSTA
> GONNA GRAB A BUNCH O'
>   RICHES

PHYLLIS.
> WHO ARE YOU?

JIMMY.
> I THE ILLEST
> I BE CATNIP TO THE
>   BITCHES
> I HAD A DREAM
> THAT I
> BE BLACK
> I A GANGSTA!

PHYLLIS.
> WHO ARE YOU?

JIMMY. Word.

> (**JIMMY** *and* **PHYLLIS** *strike a pose as song ends.*)

ERNIE. Enough! I've wasted the entire morning – fetching gum, procuring weaponry, arguing with my only son over whether or not he's black. Jimmy, go to your room.

JIMMY. But, Dad, c'mon. You my…!

ERNIE. *(putting up a hand to stop* **JIMMY***)* I am flattered you consider me your…N-word. But use it one more time and I will take this rifle and blow your damn game machine to smithereens!

JIMMY. That would be very hypocritical of you, Dad.

ERNIE. Oh, yeah? How so?

JIMMY. Because you and Mom have always raised me to be against capital punishment. Now you're threatening to kill my Game-Box?!

ERNIE. It's a machine, Jimmy, not another person.

JIMMY. IT'S MY HOMEY! Damn! Y'all can kiss my black ass!

> (**JIMMY** *storms out.*)

ERNIE. Where did he come from? How did this happen? How did he happen? This is your fault, Pam. You're far too lenient!

(exits to basement)

[*"YOU'RE THE ONLY FRIEND I'VE GOT"*]

PAM.

FALLING APART
NEED A SHOULDER TO CRY ON
TRY TO THINK OF WHO I MIGHT CALL
SOMEONE WITH HEART
OR SOME MEDS TO GET HIGH ON
WE'D GET DRUNK AND HAVE A GOOD BAWL

NOBODY HERE
WHO WILL TELL ME LOUD AND CLEAR
"THE WORLD MAY BE NUTS BUT YOU ARE NOT"
I RUN TO YOU
THOUGH OUR MEETING'S TABOO

(Quickly, she pulls out the un-smoked cigarette and sings to it.)

YOU'RE THE ONLY FRIEND I'VE GOT

(JIMMY *sings from another area with his game controller.)*

JIMMY.

FEEL SO ALONE
LIKE A RAPPER IN FARGO
I SAY "YO"
THEY GO "WHAT'S THAT MEAN?"
MOM AND DAD ACT
LIKE I'M UNWANTED CARGO
SO I HANG WITH MY GAME MACHINE

(ERNIE *is revealed singing to his guitar.)*

ERNIE.

I LOVE MY AXE
YOU SUPPLY WHAT MY LIFE LACKS
WITHOUT YOU I WOULDN'T BE THIS HOT

(PHYLLIS *is revealed, singing to a statue of Jesus.)*

PHYLLIS.

JESUS, MY MAN

> SMITE THE SMOKERS WHILE YOU CAN

PAM, ERNIE, JIMMY, PHYLLIS.
> YOU'RE THE ONLY FRIEND I'VE GOT

PAM & ERNIE.
> YOU DON'T REBEL

JIMMY & PHYLLIS.
> YOU LISTEN SO WELL

PAM, ERNIE, JIMMY, PHYLLIS.
> YOU DON'T ACT WEIRD OR STRANGE
> YOU DON'T MAKE INSANE DEMANDS
> PUT ME DOWN OR SLAP MY HANDS
> YOU NEVER TELL ME TO CHANGE

> PEOPLE ARE HARD
> SO MUCH TROUBLE TO DEAL WITH
> I CAN DO WITHOUT THEM JUST FINE

PAM.	**ERNIE, JIMMY, PHYLLIS.**
YOU KNOW I'M SCARRED	OOOOO
YOU'RE THE ONE I AM	OOOOO
REAL WITH	
'CAUSE YOU NEVER TALK	YOU NEVER WHINE
BACK OR WHINE	

PAM, ERNIE, JIMMY, PHYLLIS.
> YOU HAVE MYSTIQUE
> YOU DON'T QUESTION IF I'M WEAK
> THE DOUBTERS WHO DO CAN ALL GO ROT
> YOU HELP ME SURVIVE
> TOO BAD YOU'RE NOT ALIVE
> YOU'RE THE ONLY FRIEND I'VE GOT, YES
> YOU'RE THE ONLY FRIEND I'VE GOT

> *(Song ends. **ERNIE**, **JIMMY** and **PHYLLIS** exit. Guitar music heard from below. **PAM** puts the cigarette pack back in the cookie jar, crosses to basement door and calls down.)*

PAM. Ernie? Ernie?

ERNIE. *(offstage)* Yeah?

PAM. Could you come up here?

(The guitar playing from down below stops.)

ERNIE. Why?

PAM. JUST COME THE FUCK UP HERE! *(radical change of tone)* Please.

ERNIE. *(entering)* What's the matter?

PAM. I'm lonely. And scared. I'm not cut out for prison.

ERNIE. I don't know what else I can do to help. The resolve to quit has to come from within.

PAM. But "within" is just a big black hole longing to be filled with tar and nicotine.

ERNIE. Sweetie, I know you can do this. Just think about who you love more – tobacco or me? Me – who's behind you one hundred and thirty-eight percent. Me – who's working on a hit song which will make us rich. Me – who's got to get back to that hit song.

(turns to go)

PAM. Can I hear what you're writing?

ERNIE. Really? You want to hear my latest tune?

PAM. You know I love your music.

ERNIE. Well…it's very rough…I haven't had time to refine… *(striking a pose)* Two! Three! Fawh!

*(With that, **ERNIE** is into his rock star fantasy – flashing lights, thick haze, heavy back-up.)*

[*"STRAIGHT WHITE MAN"*]

DISABLED ASIAN LESBIANS
GET ALL KINDS OF BREAKS
IMMEDIATE FORGIVENESS
IF THEY SHOULD MAKE MISTAKES
AFFIRMATIVE REACTION
FOR ALL THEIR BELLYACHES
BUT LET A WHITE GUY
PROTEST HIS FATE
AND HE'LL BE HEARING

"YOUR PAIN DON'T RATE
YOU ARE PRIV'LEGED
AND WHAT'S MORE YOU ARE STRAIGHT!"

One, a-two, three, four!

NOBODY GOT CANDY
FOR THE STRAIGHT WHITE MAN
NOBODY GETS RANDY
FOR THE STRAIGHT WHITE MAN
THOUGH YOUR FUTURE'S AS DEPRESSING
AS A FISH IN A PAN
NOBODY IS STRESSING
FOR THE STRAIGHT WHITE MAN

(singing his own backups)

STRAIGHT WHITE MAN

Back up chicks! Big Afros. Big tits!

STRAIGHT WHITE MAN
THOSE SINGLE URBAN GRANDMOTHERS
GET HELP PAYING BILLS
GAY LATINO ADDICTS
GET HAND-OUTS OF FREE PILLS
TRANSEXUALS GET VOUCHERS
FOR PLATFORM ESPADRILLES
BUT LET A STRAIGHT DUDE
BEMOAN HIS PLIGHT
AND HE'LL BE HEARING
"YOU HAVE NO RIGHT
YOU'RE A HET'RO
YOU'RE MA-LE AND YOU'RE WHITE!"

Six, a five-six, seven, eight!

NOBODY GOT POWDER
FOR THE STRAIGHT WHITE MAN
AND NOBODY GOT CHOWDER
FOR THE STRAIGHT WHITE MAN
SO GO CRY ABOUT TOMORROW
JUST AS LOUD AS YOU CAN

BUT NOBODY GOT SORROW FOR
This is what a bad mood sounds like!

(guitar solo)

NOBODY GOT POWDER
FOR THE STRAIGHT WHITE MAN
NOBODY GOT CHOWDER
FOR THE STRAIGHT WHITE MAN

(Song ends. Lights, etc. return to normal.)

Whaddaya think?

PAM. It's…wonderful…

ERNIE. Yes! I really want your honest feed-back.

PAM. Honestly, I love it. Especially the music. Very catchy.

ERNIE. Thanks. But…you're not as crazy about the lyric?

PAM. It's…surprising. I always thought of you as such a leftie radical – like you'd be the first one out there fighting for the rights of disabled Asian lesbians. But this seems positively…reactionary.

ERNIE. Glad I can still surprise you. Thoughts about specific images?

PAM. Well…I understand "powder" as in "nobody got powder" like when you were in your coke-head phase.

ERNIE. I don't see it that literally.

PAM. Okay. I think it works. But …"chowder"? Why would a straight white man want chowder?

ERNIE. Maybe he's from New England? And…he just really wants some chowder. But nobody will give it to him because he's not from AN OPPRESSED MINORITY!

ASPHYXIA SYSTEM. *(offstage voice)* Attention! Attention! Anti-smoking technology update: AppleGoogle has announced the release of Smoke-bots…

PAM. I'm afraid to think what Smoke-bots might be.

ASPHYXIA SYSTEM. *(offstage voice)* …fierce androids programmed to smell tobacco from blocks away, even if it's buried in concrete.

(singing)

ASPHYXIA KEEPS YOU
UP-TO-DATE
ON TECHNOLOGY
THAT COULD SEAL YOUR FATE

PAM. That's it! You are going down!

(**PAM** *charges toward the ASPHYXIA but stops as* **PHYLLIS** *enters suddenly.*)

PHYLLIS. Thank the Lord you're both here. Have you heard about the Smoke-bots?

PAM. Oh yes. Ernie got us the Obnox-i-box.

PHYLLIS. Isn't technology great? Smoke Squads are already rounding up the worst offenders and putting them in Smoker's Prison.

PAM. Oh my God!

PHYLLIS. You're right, Pam. I'm sure the Lord's hand is behind this. They came for Caroline this morning.

ERNIE. Caroline? Down the block?!

PHYLLIS. Her eleven-year-old called the Squad.

PAM. That sweet little…?

PHYLLIS. She is sweet. And a good daughter. She did it for her mother's own good.

PAM. Smoker's Prison doesn't sound very good to me.

PHYLLIS. She'll live a much longer life.

PAM. In a jail cell? Is longer better in that case?

PHYLLIS. Of course it is! You are so funny sometimes. Gotta go spread the good news to those who don't have ASPHYXIA. Later.

(exits)

PAM. I can't believe it. Caroline – in jail?! Oh, Ernie, what are we going to do now?

ERNIE. "We"? I already quit. The problem isn't me.

PAM. Well the problem isn't me either! It's this country. What the hell happened to the pursuit of happiness – of that first cigarette in the morning? The freedom to choose – between Marlboros, Salems or Kents?

ERNIE. Kents?

PAM. I've heard some people like them

["FIGHT FOR THE RIGHT TO LIGHT UP"]

I THOUGHT THIS COUNTRY WAS FOUNDED
ON THE RIGHT TO PURSUE OUR OWN JOY
THE RIGHT TO SET OUR OWN STANDARDS
FOR THE CHILDREN WE DESTROY
THE RIGHT TO BE FAT AND UNHEALTHY
OR SWIM IN TOO MUCH BOOZE
THE RIGHT TO INDULGE OUR BAD HABITS
AND USE WHAT WE CHOOSE TO ABUSE

WE CAN'T BE THE ONLY PEOPLE FRIGHTENED
WHO FEAR THEY'LL HAVE TO BOLT
WE HAVE TO SEEK OUT THE MORE ENLIGHTENED
WHO WILL JOIN THE REVOLT
THOSE WHO WON'T HIDE, LIE AND COWER
SEEING BUTTS OUT THERE TO WHUP
NOW IS THE DAY AND THE HOUR
TO FIGHT FOR THE RIGHT TO LIGHT UP
Ernie, we can fight this.

ERNIE. How?

PAM. Well...for starters we'll organize the neighborhood.

ERNIE. Phyllis has already done that.

PAM. We can stage a rally at the University. A big smoke-in!

ERNIE. You'll lose your job. Everyone hates smokers.

PAM. Well, everyone used to hate goat cheese. And look how that changed!

ERNIE. How did that change?

PAM. Probably because some brave ram or ewe stood up, fought back and repositioned the product. And if no one else is willing to lead this fight, I'll be that goat!
IT'S CLEARLY TIME TO TAKE ACTION

NOT DEBATE WHETHER OTHERS WILL LEAD
REBELLION WILL NOT GAIN TRACTION
IF WE DON'T PUT ON SOME SPEED
I FEAR PAUL REVERE ISN'T RIDING
TO WARN US OF GREAT HARM
IF NOBODY ELSE SEES WHAT'S COMING
THEN I'LL HAVE TO SOUND THE ALARM

(now ready to lead the troops)

WE CAN'T LET THE FORCES OF OPPRESSION
TAKE ALL OUR RIGHTS AWAY
WE CAN'T BE THE SYMBOLS OF TRANSGRESSION
THAT THEY PUT ON DISPLAY
WE MUST BE BOLD AND NOT COWER
THERE ARE BUTTS OUT THERE TO WHUP
NOW IS THE DAY AND THE HOUR
TO FIGHT FOR THE RIGHT

ERNIE.
IT'S THE DAY AND THE HOUR
TO FIGHT FOR THE RIGHT

PAM & ERNIE.
THE DAY AND THE HOUR
TO FIGHT FOR THE RIGHT
TO LIGHT UP

PAM. Let's go! We have to start building the Resistance now!

ERNIE. All right!

PAM. We'll need survival supplies!

ERNIE. Yes!

PAM. Disguises!

ERNIE. Check.

PAM. Cell phones that can't be traced!

ERNIE. *(his enthusiasm starting to wane)* Okay.

PAM. You should start digging a bunker in the back yard. Oh, Ernie, together we'll lead the Smoker's Revolution! The Nicotine Resistance!

ERNIE. Sorry, honey, I really do have hits to write. Can you start without me?

PAM. Ernie, I can't do this alone!

ERNIE. You're not alone! I'm with you! In spirit. How long will you be gone?

PAM. I don't know. I've never organized underground cells before.

ERNIE. Love you.

(He exits to the basement. **PAM** *crosses to the cookie jar and pulls out the un-smoked cigarette.)*

PAM. *(to cigarette)* Don't worry – much as I'd like to I won't consume you – yet. Well, maybe just a puff for inspiration.

(She puts the cigarette to her lips and goes to light it.)

PHYLLIS. *(offstage)* Ernie? Ernie?

PAM. Shit!

(Realizing she's about to be caught, **PAM** *jumps into the broom closet.* **ERNIE** *enters from the basement as* **PHYLLIS** *enters.)*

ERNIE. Thank you for getting here so quickly.

PHYLLIS. I just got your text! I was making effigies of lapsers to burn at the Burn.

ERNIE. I was about to become one of those lapsers.

PHYLLIS. No! What brought this on?

ERNIE. I'm very worried about the new laws. And terrorists. The economy. Global warming.

PHYLLIS. And the Apocalypse! All the troubles you mention are signs that it's just around the corner.

ERNIE. On top of everything else, Jimmy thinks he's black.

PHYLLIS. It's a phase. They all go through it. I went through it. I feel for you, Ernie. Raising a teenager in our Godless society is a challenge. But you're doing a good job.

ERNIE. Then why do I want to paddle his little white ass until he begs for Barry Manilow's "Greatest Hits"?

PHYLLIS. Is Pam doing her share?

ERNIE. Oh, Phyllis, I shouldn't tell you this. I feel like I'm betraying my own wife. She lapsed again.

PHYLLIS. Lord! No!

ERNIE. I found her in the broom closet smoking a stub.

PHYLLIS. No, Lord, no! Not the broom closet!

ERNIE. I try to be understanding. But I have needs too! My needs have needs!

PHYLLIS. Oh, Ernie, Ernie, Ernie! What can I do?

ERNIE. Kiss me!

PHYLLIS. But Jimmy's in the other room.

ERNIE. Playing his video games. We could do each other right at his feet and he wouldn't notice.

PHYLLIS. No, Ernie! That's all over. Whenever we made love you wanted a ciggie afterward.

ERNIE. That wouldn't happen now. All I need is you. Kiss me!

PHYLLIS. No, Ernie! It's wrong. You should be making love to your wife.

ERNIE. But she reeks of tobacco! I can't spend another night on top of Old Smokey.

PHYLLIS. No, Ernie.

ERNIE. Phyllis, what would Jesus do?

PHYLLIS. Well, he certainly wouldn't kiss you, you're another boy! When I found Jesus I vowed to give up smoking and affairs with married men. The smoking was easier.

ERNIE. I couldn't have quit without your example as inspiration. Won't you let me show my appreciation?

PHYLLIS. Of course! Show your appreciation how?

ERNIE. That special thing that used to make you tingle with pleasure?

PHYLLIS. When you blew smoke up my...? It's a violation of everything I now hold dear!

ERNIE. But you loved it.

PHYLLIS. And I loved you. But that doesn't make it right.

["IF IT FEELS THIS GOOD"]

YOU'RE LIKE BACON
YOU'RE LIKE TWINKIES
YOU'RE LIKE PORK CHOPS DRIPPIN' GREASE
YES I'M ACHIN'
FOR SOME KINKIES
AS MY LUSTFUL THOUGHTS INCREASE
YOU'RE MY RED MEAT
AND MY DONUTS
THE BEST SEX I EVER HAD
IF IT FEELS THIS GOOD
IT MUST BE BAD

ERNIE.

YOU'RE LIKE NICOTINE
AND COCAINE
WHEN I USED TO DO THAT STUFF
JUST ONE CARTON
OR ONE KILO
WASN'T EVER NEAR ENOUGH
YOU'RE LIKE BLOW-JOBS
IN A WHOREHOUSE
TO A SEX-STARVED SINGLE DAD

ERNIE & PHYLLIS.

IF IT FEELS THIS GOOD
IT MUST BE BAD

IF IT FEELS THIS GOOD
IT MUST BE SATAN'S INVENTION
CAUSING MORTAL SIN
AND PERSISTENT HYPERTENSION
YOU'LL GO STRAIGHT TO HELL
YOUR SENTENCE IRONCLAD
IF IT FEELS THIS GOOD
IT MUST BE BAD

PHYLLIS.

MUST BE BAD

I'LL DO MEETINGS

ERNIE.

I'LL TAKE TWELVE STEPS

GO COLD TURKEY FROM YOUR CHARMS

PHYLLIS.

I'LL DO WORK-OUTS

ERNIE.

MEDITATION

PHYLLIS.

I'LL STICK NEEDLES IN MY ARMS

ERNIE & PHYLLIS.

BUT I'LL NEVER

KICK THE HABIT

OF YOUR TONGUE WHICH DRIVES ME MAD

IF IT FEELS THIS GOOD

IT MUST BE BAD

IF IT FEELS THIS GOOD

ANOTHER NAIL IN YOUR CASKET

YOU'LL BE MARKED WITH SIN

AND YOU'LL HAVE NO WAY TO MASK IT

WHEN YOU BURN IN HELL

YOUR SCREAMS WILL MAKE ME SAD

IF IT FEELS THIS GOOD

IT MUST BE BAD

IF IT FEELS THIS GOOD

IT MUST BE

MUST BE

MUST BE...

(They are on the island counter about to have sex. **PAM** *jumps out of the broom closet.)*

PHYLLIS. Oh, shit.

PAM. So, Phyllis, is this what Jesus would do?

ERNIE. You were in the broom closet again?

PHYLLIS. And you've hidden there before!

PAM. This is not about me! Or where I may hang out!

PHYLLIS. What is that in your hand?

PAM. This may be the last cigarette in America, Phyllis. And, you know what? I'm going to smoke it.

PHYLLIS. No!!!

ERNIE. Don't do it, honey. This is my fault.

PAM. You're right, Ernie. It is. You and this fornicatrix!

PHYLLIS. Pam, I know you're angry, but are words with a bunch of syllables necessary?

PAM. How about a mono-syllable? Slut!

ERNIE. Sweetie. Can't we keep this discourse on a more elevated level?

PAM. Ernie, how can we organize the Resistance when you're consorting with the enemy?

PHYLLIS. Resistance to what?

PAM. You and your kind, Phyllis. Everyone who won't allow me to pursue my own happiness.

JIMMY. *(entering)* What's all the yelling about?

ERNIE & PAM. Go to your room!

JIMMY. No!

PHYLLIS. Jimmy, this is an adult situation.

JIMMY. Fuck you, lady.

PHYLLIS. Okay. Well.

JIMMY. What's that, Mom? In your hand? A cigarette?

PHYLLIS. Look at what you're exposing him to, Pamela. Have you no pity?

JIMMY. Can I try it?

PAM. NO! This is mine! I've been saving it for a very special occasion. All my life I've fought the good fight. I protested against the wars. I marched for civil rights, women's rights, gay rights. I was pro-choice and anti-bigotry. I contributed to the effort to save the fuckin' owls in the Northwest timberlands and the dolphins in the sea of China. I did my part for endangered species everywhere. Well, now I'M AN ENDANGERED SPECIES! And I'm tired. And all I want is a smoke.

JIMMY. So, can I try it?

PHYLLIS. See, Pam. See.

PAM. No, Phyllis, I don't see how you can act so damned pious and be fucking my husband.

PHYLLIS. Pam! In front of your son?

PAM. You were? Jimmy, have they been fucking in front of you?

JIMMY. *(shrugging)* I was, like, playing my video games. Am I gonna have a black little brother?!!!

PHYLLIS. I can't stay here and listen to this. Pam, I will pray for you. Ernie, call the Smoke Squad.

ERNIE. She's my wife! I can't send her to Smoker's Prison!

PHYLLIS. Why not? She's clearly an add –

PAM. Don't you dare use the A-word!

PHYLLIS. Ernie, she belongs in a cell. Or in hell!

PAM. While you two debate my disposal, I'm going to light up.

ERNIE. Honey! Please. Think about your family.

PAM. That makes me want to smoke more than anything.

ERNIE. You'll be a fugitive.

PAM. So? What's keeping me here?

ERNIE. Your job?

PAM. Won't miss it a bit.

PHYLLIS. Your son?

PAM. Won't notice I'm gone.

ERNIE. Me?

(Pause. No response.)

Your husband? Honey? Me?

PAM. Doesn't deserve an answer.

ERNIE. Ohhhh! Get me the CLOWN!

PAM. Get it yourself.

ASPHYXIA SYSTEM. *(offstage voice)* Attention. Attention. Smoking penalty update.

PAM. Oooohhh! *(now throwing handfuls of cookies at* **ASPHYXIA SYSTEM***)* Ernie, where'd you put that shotgun?

ASPHYXIA SYSTEM. *(offstage voice)* Anyone caught smoking will be sentenced to a minimum of twenty years in prison.

PAM. PISS OFF! *(out of frustration, punches* **ERNIE***'s inflatable clown)*

ERNIE. Don't touch my clown!

JIMMY. Light it, Mom! I wanna see this. A terrible, horrible crime right in our own home!

PAM. Jimmy, I appreciate your support. But if I smoke this cigarette, I'll be thrown in jail. Or have to go on the lam and organize the Resistance from a remote location. Either way I won't be around anymore. Won't you miss me?

JIMMY. Can I still play my video games?

PAM. I won't be here to tell you no.

JIMMY. Then smoke it, ma!

ERNIE. Jail time, Pam!

PHYLLIS. Eternal damnation!

["THE LAST CIGARETTE"]

PAM.

> I'M AT THE END OF MY TETHER
> END OF MY ROPE
> GIVE ME A RIFLE
> OR GIVE ME SOME DOPE
> THIS SCENE IS AS HORRID
> AS ANY I'VE SEEN YET
> AND I'M DOWN TO THE LAST CIGARETTE

PHYLLIS. Pam, let's get down on our knees and pray together.

PAM. I'm sure you have lots of experience getting down on your knees but I'm not going there.

> YOU CAUSE MORE STRESS THAN A TUMOR
> GROWING INSIDE

GO SPREAD A RUMOR
GO DRINK CYANIDE
I'D MAKE YOU MY ASHTRAY
NO THOUGHT OF REGRET
BUT I'M DOWN TO THE LAST CIGARETTE

ERNIE.
I KNOW THAT YOU'RE ANGRY
I KNOW YOU'RE UPSET

PAM. You have no idea.

ERNIE.
THIS IS THE FINAL ROUND OF RUSSIAN ROULETTE
DON'T SMOKE THAT LAST CIGARETTE

JIMMY.
LIGHT IT UP, MA
THIS I GOTTA SEE
STRIKE THAT MATCH FOR ME
SOMETHING I'LL NEVER FORGET
YOU BE BLACK, YOU BE COOL
IF YOU SMOKE YOU WILL RULE
LIGHT THAT CIGARETTE

PHYLLIS.
YOU'RE HOLDING THE KEY
TO THE APOCALYPSE
THAT'S SATAN'S TOOL IN YOUR FINGERTIPS
OH THE EVIL YOU'LL BEGET
IF YOU SMOKE THAT CIGARETTE
Ernie, text the Smoke Squad. I can feel it – she's about
to blow!

ERNIE. You leave me no choice, Pam.

PAM.
HOW CAN I POSSIBLY QUIT NOW?
HOW CAN I STAY?
MAYBE IT'S BETTER IF I RUN AWAY
JAIL OR DESERTION?
THIS IS DOOMSDAY!

JIMMY. Smoke that shit, Ma!

PAM	ERNIE	JIMMY	PHYLLIS
I'M AT THE END OF MY			YOU'RE HOLDING THE
TETHER	WE CAN GET		KEY
END OF MY	THROUGH THIS		TO THE A-
ROPE	TOGETHER	Light it up!	POCALYPSE
GIVE ME A	I'LL HELP YOU		JUDGMENT
RIFLE OR	COPE		DAY
GIVE ME SOME	I'LL GIVE YOU		
DOPE	HOPE	Smoke that shit!	HOPE THAT YOU
THIS SCENE IS	DO NOT		CHOKE ON YOUR
AS HORRID AS	FRET		SMOKE
ANY I'VE SEEN	NOTHING TO		YOU'RE A
YET	SWEAT		THREAT
SEAL MY FATE		THIS IS GREAT	
WITH THIS LAST		IT'S THE LAST	
CIGARETTE		CIGARETTE	
END DEBATE	DESSICATE	LIBERATE	SATAN'S BA
WITH THIS	THAT LAST	THAT LAST	IS THAT LA!
CIGARETTE	CIGARETTE	CIGARETTE	CIGARETTE
WATCH ME SMOKE			
THE LAST			
CIGARETTE			
	LAST CIGARETTE	LAST CIGARETTE	LAST CIGARET

(**PAM** *lights up and inhales deeply. We hear sirens and Smoke-bots. A poster of* **PAM** *flies in:* "WANTED FOR SMOKING – AND SMOKEBOT EVASION." *Blackout.*)

ASPHYXIA SYSTEM. *(offstage voice)* Alert! Alert! Be on the lookout for smoking fugitives and renegades. Be sure to report any scent of tobacco lingering in the air, on clothing or especially on people's breath. Get up in their faces and scream, "Exhale into my nostrils!" And if you smell something, say something.

(Scene change to one year later. The Annual Tobacco Burn.)

PHYLLIS. *(enters in front of curtain and addresses the audience)* Welcome, welcome to our neighborhood's Annual Tobacco Burn – this year celebrating the anniversary of the introduction of the Smokebots. We especially want to welcome the newcomers we see here tonight. Welcome. Welcome. Some people don't attend because they think the problem is already solved. To them we say, "What are you smoking?!" Yes, the advertisers have been water-boarded, the vendors punished with extraordinary rendition and the manufacturers put to death! But – *(calling offstage)* Ernie?

(**ERNIE** *enters, carrying a large piece of tag board.*)

You know Ernie. Let's say "Hi."

(leads audience) Hi, Ernie!

(to audience, disappointed) Oh, come on. You can do better than that. This guy has been through hell so let's greet him like we care.

(leading audience again) Hi, Ernie!!! That's much better. Though Ernie quit smoking his life has still been nearly ruined by tobacco. Because his wife couldn't say "Get thee behind me, Nicotine." So what did she do? About a year ago now, she smoked a cigarette!

(waits for a response from the audience)

PHYLLIS. *(cont.)* I said she smoked a cigarette! Let's hear some approbation!

(leads the audience in booing)

Boo! Then she deserted her supportive husband and abandoned her adorable only child.

(Again gets audience to boo. Then calls offstage.) Boo! Jimmy?

(Pause. No response. Now firmly –)

JIMMY!!!

(JIMMY stumbles on like a zombie, carrying another piece of tagboard.)

Poor, innocent, little Jimmy was so traumatized by his mother's flight from justice that his medications had to be triple-dosed.

JIMMY. *(not too forceful, he's zonked)* Booooo.

PHYLLIS. I wish his mother was here to see what her sin has done to her family. I wish her lungs could talk and tell her how much she's hurt them. Ernie, show us the picture of a healthy lung.

(ERNIE turns the piece of tagboard around revealing a graphic photo of a healthy lung – not exactly lovely.)

If that lung could talk, what would it say, Ernie?

ERNIE. It would say, "Thank you for keeping me healthy."

PHYLLIS. Yes it would! Now, Jimmy, show us your photo of a lung attacked by tobacco.

(no response)

Jimmy?

(No response. Yelling.)

JIMMY!!! *(aside)* Get it together!

*(He is chewing on the tagboard. **PHYLLIS** takes it from him and gives it to **ERNIE** to hold. It displays a disgusting lung.)*

[*"IF OUR LUNGS COULD ONLY TALK"*]

PHYLLIS. Isn't that appalling and sad? I love this next part because we ask you to speak for the lungs who can't speak for themselves. And, of course, what they'd say is "Help! Help! Help!" So whenever you hear me sing:

(sings)

HELP! HELP! HELP!
You answer with:
HELP! HELP! HELP!
Let's try it once, shall we? Here goes:

(sings)

HELP! HELP! HELP!

(gestures for audience to join)

HELP! HELP! HELP!
That's much better than last year! Now let's divide it up, okay? Starting with the men.

(sings)

IF OUR LUNGS COULD ONLY TALK
THE MANLY LUNGS WOULD SAY

*(indicates for **ERNIE** to lead the men in the audience)*

ERNIE.

HELP! HELP! HELP!

(leading the men)

HELP! HELP! HELP!

PHYLLIS. Wonderful, guys! Very manly. Okay, girls, let's show 'em what we've got.

(sings)

IF OUR LUNGS COULD ONLY TALK
THE LADIES' LUNGS WOULD CRY
HELP! HELP! HELP!

(leading the women)

HELP! HELP! HELP!

PHYLLIS. *(cont.)* Stop! That was pretty good. Except for you, Ma'am. Yes, you back there. I didn't see you singing. May I remind you we have Smokebots outside ready to arrest anyone who smokes – or doesn't sing along! So, ladies, let's try it again and hope Miss "I-Don't-Feel-Like-Singing" finds her inner songbird. Okay? Five! Six! Seven!

(sings)

IF OUR LUNGS COULD ONLY TALK
THE LADIES' LUNGS WOULD CRY
HELP! HELP! HELP!

(leading the women)

HELP! HELP! HELP!
Much better! Now, all the children.

PHYLLIS & ERNIE. *(singing)*
IF OUR LUNGS COULD ONLY TALK
THE KIDDIES' LUNGS WOULD SHRIEK

*(They look to **JIMMY** who's snoring. **PHYLLIS** kicks him.)*

JIMMY. *(coming to, but out of rhythm)* HEEEELLLPPPPP!

PHYLLIS. *(Ushering/pushing him offstage. **ERNIE** follows.)* You little mothafucka!

(back to audience)

What fun! Now let's give it a big wind-up with everybody!

IF OUR LUNGS COULD ONLY TALK
ALL OUR LUNGS WOULD SCREAM
HELP! HELP! HELP!

(leading the audience)

HELP! HELP! HELP!
HELP! HELP! HELP!

(cuing the audience)

HELP! HELP! HELP!
Big finish!
HELP! HELP! HELP!

(cuing the audience)

HELP! HELP! HELP!

(blackout)

ASPHYXIA SYSTEM. *(offstage voice)*
WE NEED YOUR HELP TO CONQUER CRIME
LET'S SEE OUTLAWS ALL DO TIME
SNIFF THEM OUT, SMELL THEIR BREATH
SMOKERS SPREAD DISEASE AND DEATH

(A few weeks later. The kitchen is in complete darkness. Then, the refrigerator door opens, the light from it falling across the stage. A shadowy figure voraciously raids the fridge.)

*(Light floods the stage. **JIMMY** has entered and switched on the lights. He is wearing Pam's bathrobe and high-heeled mules. He carries the shotgun seen earlier and points it toward the intruder at the fridge.)*

JIMMY. Don't move! I've got a gun. I said don't move! Now – back it up. Real slow. Hands in the air.

*(**PAM**, shabbily dressed in a hat and woodsman's wear which could easily cause her to be mistaken for a man, steps forward.)*

PAM. Jimmy?

JIMMY. Mom?

PAM. Oh, honey, I've missed you so much!

JIMMY. Gun! Gun! I've got a gun!!!

PAM. Jimmy, did you forget to take your medication?

JIMMY. Where have you been for the last year?

PAM. Put down the gun and I'll try to explain.

JIMMY. But I'm on watch. Dad assigned me to night duty this week!

PAM. What are you doing in my bathrobe? And heels?

JIMMY. I'm exploring my feminine side. Someone has to supply a womanly presence in this house.

PAM. Let me get you your meds.

JIMMY. I flushed 'em after people said I was a zombie at the last Burn. And they make it hard to walk in your heels.

PAM. How about this? Put that gun down and I'll give you a cookie?

JIMMY. Okay!

PAM. That's a good boy.

(She hugs him.)

JIMMY. It hasn't been the same around here without you yelling at me.

PAM. I've missed yelling at you too.

JIMMY. Now I can eat cookies, play video games whenever I want, listen to rap music.

(rapping)

I CAN BE BLACK AGAIN
NOW THAT YOU BACK AGAIN

PAM. Just like the old days.

JIMMY. So why'd you come back?

PAM. Oh, honey, life on the run is awful. I can't believe how much I missed all this – even your father, even his music. The one thing that kept me going was knowing that some day I'd come back for you.

(music in)

[*"THE LAST SMOKER IN AMERICA"*]

FIRST I WANT TO SAY I ALWAYS LOVED YOU
WHEN I LEFT I THOUGHT MY HEART WOULD BREAK
SOMETIMES WE FEEL PASSION
WAY BEYOND OUR CONTROL
CONSTANT CRAVING IS IMPOSSIBLE TO SHAKE

I'M THE LAST SMOKER IN AMERICA
'CAUSE ALL THE REST GOT CANCER OR DID TIME
THE LAST SMOKER IN AMERICA
HOW MUCH MUST I SUFFER FOR MY CRIME?

I'VE BEEN ON THE RUN ONE YEAR AND COUNTING
HOOKED UP WITH SOME RENEGADES I MET

WE WERE CHASED BY BLOODHOUNDS
AND BY SMOKE-BOTS
THEY GOT MY PALS
AND STUBBED OUT MY LAST CIGARETTE

I'M THE LAST SMOKER IN AMERICA
IT'S NOT LIKE I DO HEROIN OR CRANK
THE LAST SMOKER IN AMERICA
WISH I ONLY OVERATE OR DRANK

AND YOU HAVE SEEN
HOW I TRIED TO QUIT
COLD TURKEY AND PATCHES AND NIC-A
CARCINOGENS
WOULDN'T MANUMIT
COULDN'T BREAK THE FILTHY HABIT
SO I MADE MY GET-AWAY

NOW I'VE REACHED THE END OF BUTTS AND FILTERS
ONLY WANT TO EAT UNTIL I GAG
MAYBE WE SHOULD TRY TO FLEE THE COUNTRY?
I BET IN ENGLAND I COULD SOMEHOW SNAG A FAG

(**JIMMY** sings back-up as do **ERNIE** and **PHYLLIS**, who enter through the cabinets dressed as patriots of the American Revolution.)

PAM.	**JIMMY, ERNIE, PHYLLIS.**
	SNAG A FAG
I'M THE LAST SMOKER IN AMERICA	AHHH-MER-I-CA
HAS ANYBODY KNOWN A SADDER LOT?	AHH A SADDER LOT
THE LAST SMOKER IN AMERICA	THE LAST SMOKER IN AMERICA
MAYBE I SHOULD TAKE UP SMOKING POT!	AHHHH
YES I AM THE LAST SMOKER IN AMERICA	LAST SMOKER IN AMERICA
AND NOW MY LIFE IS NOT WORTH	AHHHH
DIDDLY-SQUAT	
NOT DIDDLY-SQUAT	NOT DIDDLY-SQUAT

(**ERNIE** *and* **PHYLLIS** *exit as song ends.*)

PAM. Where's your father?

JIMMY. Asleep. He's been putting in long hours as the area manager for the *(spelling it out)* N.A.T.C.

PAM. Oh, I'm so happy he finally found a job. What is N.A.T.C.?

JIMMY. Neighborhood Anti-Tobacco Crusade – NATC.

(pronounced like "Nazi")

PAM. Shit.

(**ERNIE** *enters. His look is much more conservative and cleaned up – hair slicked-back, etc. He is wearing pajamas.*)

PAM. Oh, honey…

ERNIE. Pam?

PAM. I'm home.

ERNIE. PAM! What the – ?!

(He starts "Riverdancing" – furiously doing Irish-jig type steps.)

PAM. What are you doing?

JIMMY. It's his new anger management technique – working out his rage through Riverdancing.

PAM. The clown wasn't working?

JIMMY. He shot it. Smoking was so much healthier for him

PAM. Ernie, please. We have to forget the past and move on. I really need your help.

ERNIE. *(still dancing)* A good citizen always offers his neighbor a helping hand.

PAM. Neighbor!? What's wrong with you?

ERNIE. Nothing's wrong with me.

(picking up the rifle and handing it to **JIMMY***)*

Jimmy, shoot your mother.

JIMMY. No way.

ERNIE. Ever since you left, he's been worse than ever. Never takes his medication. Rebels against my every order. Never mind, Jimmy. I'll shoot your mother.

PAM. NOOO! Ernie, please. We loved each other. Remember the smoky bar? The red neon glow? The crappy service? Back before…before you got this way.

ERNIE. This way? Other men whose wives left them for a tobacco fix might have gotten a little down.

PAM. I didn't leave you for a tobacco fix! You were fucking Phyllis!

ERNIE. Other men might have gotten violent. Not me. Before I was shown the frivolousness of my rock star dreams I wrote a song about you. Wanna hear it?

PAM. Ernie, this is neither the time nor place – We're in the middle of a crisis!

(music in – lilting, folkie strumming)

ERNIE. Shhh! Let it wash over you.

[*"I WANNA CALL YOU –"*]

OUR HOUSE RANG
WITH PET NAMES OF AFFECTION
"BABE" AND "SWEETIE"
ECHOED THOUGH THE PLACE
EACH MONIKER
A SUGARY CONFECTION
LIKE A COOKIE
WITH A HAPPY SMILEY FACE

THEN YOU LEFT
AND ALL THE ROOMS GREW QUIET
OH THE SOUR TASTE
THAT STAYED BEHIND
YOU REMOVED THE SUGAR
FROM MY DIET
AND NAMES THAT AREN'T AS SWEET
NOW COME TO MIND

(music turns hard)

I WANNA CALL YOU THE C-WORD

EVEN THOUGH THAT WOULD BE WRONG
I WANNA CALL YOU THE C-WORD
THOUGH IT'S NOT PRETTY IN A SONG
I TRY TO MANAGE MY ANGER
I TRY TO SMILE AND BLUFF
BUT I STILL WANNA CALL YOU THE C-WORD
'CAUSE BITCH FACE AIN'T STRONG ENOUGH!

I WANNA CALL YOU AN ASSHOLE
BUT IT LACKS A CERTAIN BITE
I WANNA CALL YOU A DICK-HEAD
BUT GUESS THE GENDER ISN'T RIGHT
AND IF YOU WEREN'T A FEMALE
I'D SAY YOU WERE A PRICK
SO I STILL WANNA CALL YOU THE C-WORD
'CAUSE ASS WIPE WON'T DO THE TRICK!

(He riffs.)

PAM. Ernie. Ernie!!

*(**ERNIE** stops riffing.)*

What kind of song is that?!!

ERNIE. Classic rock with an Emo flair. In the midst of writing it, Phyllis appeared in a vision and showed me how to channel my rage.

*(**PHYLLIS** appears like a vision out of County Cork – Tam o'Shanter, kilt – total Irish lass drag. She sings a jaunty Irish jig-style ditty.)*

PHYLLIS.

YOU NEED TO LEARN
THE TRICK OF THE IRISH
THEY USE WHEN TEMPERS FLARE
YOU NEED TO DANCE
THE JIGS OF THE IRISH
PUT ALL YOUR ANGER THERE

AND EVEN THOUGH
THERE'S NO HINT OF IRISH
IN YOUR WHOLE FAM'LY TREE
I KNOW YOU'LL DIG

AN IRISH JIG
WITH A COMELY LASS LIKE ME!

(She teaches **ERNIE** *to "Riverdance." Fiercely. Then gets* **JIMMY** *to join. At the end of dance break, she disappears.)*

ERNIE. *(erupting again upon seeing* **PAM***)*
I WANNA CALL YOU A DOUCHE-BAG
SAY A STRING OF NASTY THINGS
I WANNA CALL YOU A SKANK WHORE
BUT I'M NOT CERTAIN IF IT SINGS
I TRY TO MANAGE MY ANGER
I TRY TO SMILE AND BLUFF
BUT I STILL WANNA CALL YOU THE C-WORD
'CAUSE BEE-ATCH
AND DICK WEED!
AND ASS WIPE!
AND TAR LUNG!
AND JUNK FACE!
AND BUTT END!
AND CROTCH ROT!
AND PIE HOLE!
AND FUCK TARD!
AIN'T STRONG ENOUGH!

(song ends)

Well, Pam?

PAM. I don't think it'll get much airplay.

ERNIE. You hear the greatest fucking song since "MacArthur Park" and that's all you can say?!

PAM. I never got "left the cake out in the rain" either. Your new song is offensive.

ERNIE. I'll tell you what's offensive – mothers who desert their children!

PAM. Jimmy, is that what you think I did? Would it have been better for you if I went to jail?

JIMMY. I might have met some rappers.

*(***PHYLLIS*** enters, wearing pajamas which match **ERNIE**'s and bunny slippers.)*

PHYLLIS. Honey, was I dreaming? I thought I heard you singing and playing that song you wrote with Satan?

PAM. Phyllis?

PHYLLIS. Holy shit! Is that you Pamela? *(looking her over)* Time has not been kind.

JIMMY. *(to PAM)* I told you Dad was desperate for a female presence. *(choking up with tears of frustration)* I do what I can.

PHYLLIS. Jimmy, Jesus doesn't like you running around like a godless transvestite.

JIMMY. How would you know? Did you talk to him?

PAM. I'm sure she talks to Jesus constantly. Do you ever discuss his feelings on adultery, Phyllis?

ERNIE. Pam, let's not get personal.

PAM. Ernie, who are you? What happened to my rocker? The party animal I used to love?

PHYLLIS. He grew up, Pamela – put aside childish things.

PAM. Honey, your music isn't childish! That song is bitter and mean but I understand your anger and appreciate you channeling it into your music. How could you give that up? I know you love it. I love it!

ERNIE. Really? I never quite believed that.

PAM. When I was hiding in that cave in the woods, I used to sing all your songs to myself.

(singing plaintively)

NOBODY GOT POWDER
FOR THE STRAIGHT WHITE MAN
AND NOBODY GOT CHOWDER
FOR THE STRAIGHT WHITE MAN

ERNIE. I thought you hated that lyric.

PAM. Not after long nights of analyzing it! "Powder" and "chowder" are both white – at least if the chowder is cream-based – white like the "straight white man." It's brilliant, Ernie, brilliant.

ERNIE. I always kind of thought it was.

PHYLLIS. *(collapsing)* I can't see! I can't see! Don't listen to her! The devil's music is the doorbell to hell.

PAM. Are you the Taliban?

PHYLLIS. Somebody call an exorcist. That's Satan talking!

PAM. No, it's me, Phyllis. Ernie, sweetie, I'm back. We can be a family again.

PHYLLIS. Ernie has a family. You addict!!

(**PAM** *lunges at* **PHYLLIS**, *clawing, scratching, pulling her hair and choking her as they roll around on the floor.*)

PAM. ARRRRGGGGGHHHHHH!

JIMMY. Get her, Mom! Get her good!

ERNIE. Shut up, Jimmy! Pam, stop it!

(*pulling* **PAM** *off of* **PHYLLIS**)

This is ridiculous, Pam. You're as bad as Jimmy.

PAM. Let me go so I can kill that bitch.

(**PHYLLIS** *grabs* **ERNIE**'s *guitar and is about to smash it over* **PAM**'s *head.*)

ERNIE. Phyllis! No! Not my axe!

(*He grabs the guitar away from her.*)

Phyllis, have you lost your mind? You were about to harm an innocent…guitar?!

PHYLLIS. As Pam was trying to strangle me just now, Jesus appeared and showed me the truth – you white people are crazy!

ERNIE. Pot to kettle! Phyllis, I've tried so hard. I'm sorry. I guess I'm just not meant to be upstanding. I'm meant to get down! And rock out!

(**PAM** *and* **JIMMY** *cheer.*)

JIMMY. Yo, Dad!

PAM. That's my guy!

PHYLLIS. So this is what it's come to? Ernie, I'm beyond disappointed.

ERNIE. Phyllis…

PHYLLIS. Stop. I need a private moment with the Man Upstairs. *(prays silently)* Okay! I've been given a bigger mission than saving your sorry-assed soul.

(She grabs a tote bag and starts filling it with what's at hand – food, house plants, cleaning solvents, toilet paper – cleaning out the cabinets and closets as she rants.)

PHYLLIS. *(cont.)* Somebody has to fix our government! Or get rid of it entirely. They get all namby-pamby about executing people. Instead of just stoning heretics to death, or impaling homosexuals on hot steel rods, they want to form a committee, debate a bill, put it up for a vote. Big government has no place in these intimate decisions. That's between us and our weapons. The terrorists, jihadists and underpants bombers have taught me one important lesson: "Death to the Infidels!!!"

(She starts to the door, then turns back.)

Don't misinterpret my leave-taking as some kind of victory, Pam. My brothers and sisters will always be here – at least until we're pulled up to heaven in the Rapture and your sorry smoking butt descends to hell. GO TEAM JESUS!!

(Exits in a flourish. The others are silent for a minute.)

PAM. Gee, we're gonna have to do a shopping run. Honey, now that she's gone, I'm willing to try to make it work.

JIMMY. Hear that, Dad? We can be a family again.

PAM. Maybe not perfect.

JIMMY. Maybe not even very good…

ERNIE. Pam, you really think we can start again?

PAM. I know we can! Someplace else. What do you know about East Timor?

JIMMY. I know I don't want to go there!

PAM. Jimmy, we're all going to have to make some sacrifices.

ERNIE. Your mother's right, son. She's still a wanted criminal. We'll have to emigrate, start anew. It doesn't really matter where we go. Our lives will be so much better now that she's given up smoking.

PAM. Well…I haven't smoked for a long time because there weren't any cigarettes, but…

ERNIE. But we can be the happiest, ex-patriot, smoke-free family anywhere!

PAM. Smoke free? Who said anything about smoke free? There are still countries where it's okay to smoke. And we have to move to one of them.

ERNIE. Woman, what shit are you on?

PAM. I'm taking action! Wherever we end up I'm going to fight for the legalization of medical tobacco!

ERNIE. Pam, for Christ's sake!

PAM. Anger management, Ernie.

ERNIE. FUCK ANGER MANAGEMENT! *(grabs shotgun)* Obviously the only way to cure your problem is to shoot you!

(Suddenly JIMMY *wrenches the gun from* ERNIE*'s hands.)*

JIMMY. Nobody is shooting shit! What is wrong with you people?

PAM. Jimmy, put that gun down before someone gets hurt.

JIMMY. Gets hurt? I am hurt! I'm going to have to work the rest of my life to pay for therapy for what you two have done to me.

ERNIE. You're right, son. I've been too focused on my music career and your mother – well, your mother is a disgusting addict.

PAM. How dare you!

ERNIE. Addict! Addict!!

[*"SMOKING MAKES ME HAPPY"*]

PAM. Addict?

You call me an addict?

I'M NOT AN ADDICT

PHYLLIS. *(cont.)* How dare you say that!

> I LOVE TOBACCO
> MORE THAN IS HEALTHY
> I KNOW IT'S NOT HEALTHY
> BUT NEITHER'S TRANS-FAT
>
> YET PEOPLE WHO GORGE ON
> TOO MUCH FAST FOOD
> DON'T GO TO PRISON
> BECAUSE THEY PURSUED
> THE SHIT THAT MAKES THEM HAPPY
> SMOKING MAKES ME HAPPY!!

ERNIE. But Pam…what about me? What about your family?

PAM.

> FAM'LY?
> WE VENERATE FAM'LY
> "LIVE FOR YOUR FAM'LY"
> NO LONGER MY PLAN
> I'M THROUGH WITH OTHERS
> I WANT SOME ME TIME
> NOW IS THE TIME TO
> BECOME MY OWN MAN

JIMMY. But, Mom, you're not a man!

PAM. Shut up, Jimmy

> WHEN I STOP TO THINK
> OF WHAT HAS COME TO PASS
> LET EVERYONE KISS
> MY SMOKE-LOVING ASS
> I'LL DO WHAT MAKES ME HAPPY
> SMOKING MAKES ME HAPPY!

ERNIE. But, Pam…what about all our years together?

PAM.

> WE CAN'T RETURN TO THAT SMOKY BAR
> BUT I'LL FIND MY OWN HOWEVER FAR
> YOU'LL BE JUST FINE WITH YOUR DAMNED GUITAR
> YOU LOVE IT –
>
> WE'RE TALKING ABOUT ADDICTION?

YOU'VE GOT A LOT OF YOUR OWN
CHOCK FULL OF SUCH CONTRADICTION
I'M AMAZED
I AM DAZED
YOUR HYPROCRACY HAS MADE ME CRAZED

YOU'VE ALWAYS BEEN ADDICTED TO YOUR ROCK STAR
    DREAMS
AS YOU WERE TO OUR NEIGHBOR'S ORGASMIC SCREAMS
AND YOU STILL ARE ADDICTED TO THOSE ENERGY DRINKS
SO THIS HOLIER-THAN-THOU
"I SIMPLY WON'T ALLOW
GOTTA GIVE UP SMOKING NOW"
ALL OF IT
THE GALL OF IT
ALL OF IT STINKS!

YET YOU HAVE GOT THE NERVE TO POINT
AND SAY THAT I'M AN ADDICT?
LIKE THE REST OF THE WORLD
YOU'VE BECOME A FANATIC
YOU AND ALL THE OTHERS GET SO OPERATIC
WEEPY AND CREEPY AND OVER DRAMATIC
THEN YOU TURN AROUND AND GET ALL DULL AND
    BUREAURCRATIC
BECAUSE I LOVE TOBACCO IS IT AXIOMATIC
THAT I HAVE AN ADDICTION?
OR SOME MORAL AFFLICTION?
THAT'S A PARANOID FICTION!
DON'T ADDICTS DIE IF THEY DON'T GET THEIR FIX?
OR GO INTO CONVULSIONS IF THEY DON'T GET THEIR
    KICKS?
WELL I HAVEN'T SMOKED IN A YEAR
AND I'M HERE
SO IT'S CLEAR
I AM NOT AN ADDICT!

BUT WHEN I FIND SOME TOBACCO IT WILL MAKE ME
    ECSTATIC
'CAUSE IT'S GONNA BE RICH AND SUPER AROMATIC

GONNA SPLIT FROM YOU PEOPLE WHO ARE CRAZY
   DOGMATIC
FUNDAMENTAL, JUDGMENTAL AND TOO THEOCRATIC
MY LEAVE-TAKING MIGHT BE RUDELY SCHISMATIC
BUT THIS SO CALLED ADDICT IS GOING NOMADIC!

FUTURE?
I LOOK AT THE FUTURE
WHAT KIND OF FUTURE
IS LIFE WITHOUT SMOKE?

SO I'LL LIVE LONGER
WITHOUT TOBACCO
I'D RATHER DIE FROM
A PRE-MATURE STROKE

I KNOW I'LL FIND PEACE
ON MY BED OF DEATH
'CAUSE I'LL BE INHALING
WITH MY FINAL BREATH
AND THAT WILL MAKE ME HAPPY
SMOKING MAKES ME HAPPY!
SMOKING MAKES ME HAPPY!
SMOKING MAKES ME HAPPY!
HAPPY, HAPPY, HAPPY, HAPPY
SMOKING MAKES ME HAPPY!

ERNIE. Well, you've certainly made everything crystal clear, Pam. It kills me that you'd choose your dirty, filthy habit over us. But now I see you're right. And I want to follow your example.

PAM. You mean fighting for the legalization of medical tobacco?

ERNIE. Not that example. Freedom, Pam. Freedom. You've shown me it's more important than anything. If I have to break the law, ruin other people's lives, climb over the bodies of the family I destroyed to get where I want to go – that's okay! And I want to go out West. Start a new band. A neo-anti-smoking group that will shake this country out of its complacency.

PAM. What complacency? I'm the last smoker in America.

ERNIE. Quit stomping on my dreams!

(sings)

THE PEOPLE WILL COME FLOCKIN'
EV'RY ONE A FAN
THIS COUNTRY WILL BE ROCKIN'
TO THIS STRAIGHT WHITE MAN!!

(exits)

PAM. Whew. I think we could both use a cookie.

ASPHYXIA SYSTEM. *(offstage voice)* Attention! ASPHYXIA has been reprogrammed to expand its mission. In an effort to reduce childhood obesity, cookies have been outlawed.

JIMMY. Cookies!!! *(picks up the gun)* This time you've gone too far!

(fires at the ASPHYXIA, which falls, hanging by a cord)

ASPHYXIA SYSTEM. *(offstage voice)* Danger! Anger mismanagement!

(singing)

CALL YOUR SPONSOR
CALL YOUR SPONSOR
CALL YOUR SPONSOR
CALL YOUR SPONSOR
Fatal error! Fatal error! Fatal error! Fatal error! Fatal errorrrrrrrr ...

(ASPHYXIA system dies dramatically.)

PAM. Oh, Jimmy. I'm so proud of you. I'll help you lead the fight against cookie fascism.

(offstage the sound of distant sirens)

Phyllis must have alerted the Smoke Squad. We've got to get out of here!

JIMMY. We?

PAM. I can't leave you again.

JIMMY. But where would we go?

PAM. Kazakhstan.

JIMMY. Kazakhstan?!

PAM. They'll always smoke there. Without filters! Come on. I'm doing this for you.

JIMMY. For me?

PAM. Yes – for you. For everyone who still believes in the right to choose.

JIMMY. Choose what?

PAM. To kill themselves with whatever the hell makes them happy. We have to go now!

JIMMY. I don't want to go to Kazakhstan! Not when I'm about to start a new career.

PAM. What? What career?

JIMMY. Designing video games for black men trapped in white women's clothes.

PAM. Jimmy, for once just do as you're told.

JIMMY. No!

[*"SECOND HAND SMOKE"*]

I DON'T WANT
YOUR SECOND HAND SMOKE
SECOND-HAND CANCER
OR SECOND-HAND STROKE
I WANNA LIFE
WHERE MY NEEDS COME FIRST
THAT'S NOT GONNA HAPPEN WITH YOU

PAM. Jimmy…

JIMMY.

YOU'RE JUST LIKE
A SECOND-HAND CAR
YOU'VE KEPT ME GOING
BUT WON'T TAKE ME FAR
NOW I GET WORRIED
'BOUT SAFETY AND FUMES
'CAUSE SECOND-HAND'S DANGEROUS TOO

SECOND HAND SMOKE
SECOND HAND GOODS

I WON'T BREATHE BETTER
IN NEW NEIGHBORHOODS
YOU WERE MY GLUE
BUT THEN SOMETHING BROKE
I WON'T BE EXPOSED
TO SECOND-HAND SMOKE

PAM. You're right, Jimmy. I haven't always been there, but I'll make it up to you. How about this?

I WON'T SMOKE WHEN YOU'RE IN THE ROOM
WHY SHOULD YOU SUFFER
FOR WHAT I CONSUME?
I'LL TRY TO FIX
THE MISTAKES I HAVE MADE
AND ALL OF THE CHANCES I BLEW
No?

JIMMY & PAM.

SECOND-HAND SMOKE
SECOND-HAND DREAMS
SOMEHOW HAVE LED US
TO PAINFUL EXTREMES
YOU SAY GOODBYE
AND I START TO CHOKE

PAM.

BUT YOU WILL NOT MISS   **JIMMY.**

I WILL NOT MISS

PAM & JIMMY.

THE SECOND-HAND SMOKE

(offstage sound of sirens getting closer)

JIMMY.

I'M GONNA MAKE VIDEO GAMES

PAM.

I'VE GOTTA RUN!

JIMMY.

LOTS OF EXPLOSIONS
AND GUNS THAT THROW FLAMES

PAM.

> YOU'RE A GOOD SON
> SELL WHAT YOU CAN
> AND BUY WHAT YOU
> WANT

JIMMY.

> I'M GONNA BUY
> REALLY COOL SHIT!

PAM.

> I'LL MISS YOU
> BUT I UNDERSTAND

> SECOND-HAND SMOKE

> SECOND-HAND DREAMS
> SOMEHOW HAVE LED US
> TO PAINFUL EX…

> SOMEHOW HAVE LED US
> TO PAINFUL EX…

(PHYLLIS suddenly enters, wearing a bulky coat. PAM and JIMMY stop singing in mid-phrase, but the music continues under the following.)

PAM. Phyllis? I thought you were gone.

PHYLLIS. I have unfinished business. Where's Ernie?

PAM. He left. For good.

PHYLLIS. Damnation! I prayed you'd all be here.

JIMMY. I liked it better when you were gone.

PHYLLIS. Don't worry, Jimmy. I'm not staying.

(Various beeps and buzzes are heard offstage.)

JIMMY. What's that sound?

PAM. Smokebots!

PHYLLIS. The house is surrounded.

PAM. Jimmy, we've gotta go!

PHYLLIS. We're all going, Pam. Together.

(takes off her coat to reveal a suicide bomber vest)

JIMMY. What the fuck?!

PHYLLIS. That's some of the last smut to ever come out of your potty-mouth. I'm a charter member of Jihad for Jesus! My reward is waiting in paradise. And with the apocalypse around the corner, I'm gonna be first in line!

SECOND-HAND SMOKE
SECOND-HAND LIVES
NO SECOND CHANCES
WHEN DOOMSDAY ARRIVES
DREAMED YOU WERE GONE
BUT THEN I AWOKE
THIS IS GOODBYE
TO SECOND-HAND...

JIMMY. NO!

(**JIMMY** *tries to tackle* **PHYLLIS**. *But she pulls a cord on the vest before he knocks her down. Blinding white light and the sound of a huge explosion which bleeds into the roar of a rock concert crowd. Then hazily, through much smoke, a spotlight picks up* **ERNIE**, *who crosses to a microphone. He is now dressed like the rock star he's always imagined himself as.*)

ERNIE. How' everybody doin'! Wooo, yeah! I'm honored to be here tonight. I started living and working out West before the smoking wars even began. So to be invited to be part of this benefit for survivors of those wars is truly gratifying. Three people who were very dear to me perished in the troubles. And this song is for them – "The Ballad of the Last Smoker in America."

*[**"THE LAST SMOKER IN AMERICA" – REPRISE**]*

ONCE THERE WAS A SAD TOBACCO USER
AND I WILL ADMIT SHE WAS MY WIFE
THOUGH SHE PROVED HER HUSBAND'S WORST ABUSER
I STOOD BESIDE HER AS I TRIED TO SAVE HER LIFE

(**PAM** *and* **JIMMY** *appear as angels.*)

ERNIE.
THE LAST SMOKER IN AMERICA

PAM.
AT LEAST I DIDN'T HAVE TO COMPROMISE

PAM, JIMMY, ERNIE.
THE LAST SMOKER IN AMERICA

(**PHYLLIS** *enters as a devil with horns and tail.*)

PHYLLIS.

THERE'S STILL GAYS AND JEWS TO DEMONIZE

ERNIE.

YES SHE WAS THE

PAM, JIMMY, ERNIE, PHYLLIS.

LAST SMOKER IN AMERICA!

WE'RE WHO WE ARE AND WON'T APOLOGIZE

ERNIE.

NOW THERE ARE NO SMOKERS LEFT

PAM, JIMMY, ERNIE, PHYLLIS.

IN AMERICA!

THE END